Pride

A Level Three Reader

By Kathryn Kyle

The Child's World®

On the cover...
This boy is showing pride in the trophy he won.

Published by The Child's World®, Inc.
PO Box 326
Chanhassen, MN 55317-0326
800-599-READ
www.childsworld.com

Special thanks to the Davis, Giroux, Melaniphy, Snyder, and Toral families,
and to the staff and students of Alessandro Volta and Shoesmith Elementary
Schools for their help and cooperation in preparing this book.

Photo Credits
© Bettmann/CORBIS: 22, 25
© David Young-Wolff/PhotoEdit: 3
© Elyse Lewin/Image Bank: 6
© Romie Flanagan: 5, 9, 10, 13, 14, 17, 18, 21
© Steve Dunwell/Image Bank: cover
© Tom McCarthy/Unicorn Stock Photos: 26

Project Coordination: Editorial Directions, Inc.
Photo Research: Alice K. Flanagan

Library of Congress Cataloging-in-Publication Data
Kyle, Kathryn.
Pride / by Kathryn Kyle.
     p. cm. — (An Easy reader)
Summary: Easy-to-read scenarios, such as doing well on a test or playing
well in a soccer game, provide lessons in being proud of yourself.
ISBN 1-56766-091-6 (alk. paper)
1. Self-esteem—Juvenile literature.
[1. Self-esteem.] I. Title. II. Wonder books (Chanhassen, Minn.)
BJ1533.S3 K95 2002
152.4—dc21
                          2001007955

What is pride? Pride is feeling good about yourself and others. When we feel that way, we say that we are feeling proud.

At school, you take a math test. It is a very hard test. But you have studied a long time for the test. You get all the answers right. Pride is feeling good about how you did on the test.

You love to play soccer. You play on a soccer team. You practice hard so you can be a better player. In a game, you score a goal for your team. Pride is feeling excited about scoring the goal and helping your team.

When you feel pride, you feel good about yourself. You take time each day to get ready for school. You comb your hair and put on clean clothes. You want to look your best. Pride is feeling good about how you look.

9

You are learning to ride a skateboard. You practice every day. You are getting better, but you still fall down. You do not get upset when you fall. Instead, you keep practicing to get better. Pride is about feeling good that you are learning.

Your mother's birthday is coming soon. You go shopping to find her a birthday present. You find a perfect present. She is so pleased when she opens the present. Pride is feeling excited that you gave your mother a present she loves.

13

Your little brother wants to count to ten. You practice with him over and over. It takes patience! Finally, he learns to count to ten. You are proud of your brother because he learned something new. You are proud of yourself because you helped him do it.

You can also feel pride about where you live. When you say the **Pledge of Allegiance** to the American flag, you feel proud to live in the United States. You feel lucky to live in this country.

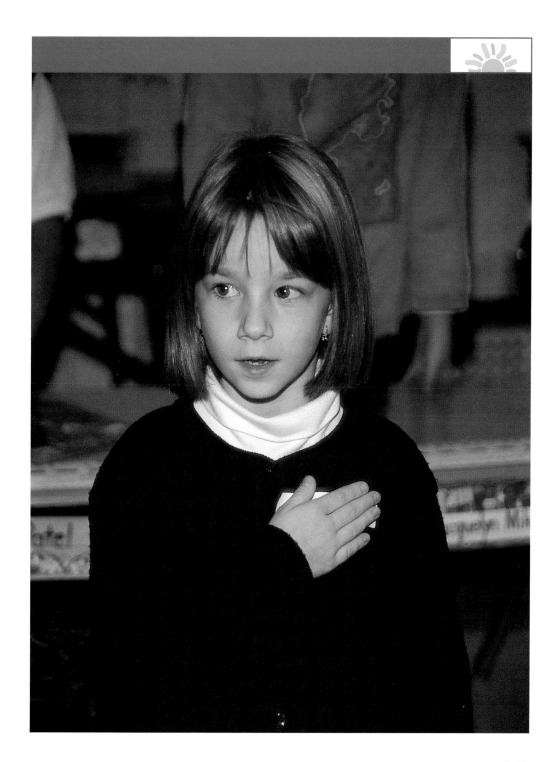

18

Your brother is in the **spelling bee** at school. He is very good at spelling. He wins first place in the spelling bee. Pride is feeling happy about what your brother has done.

Feeling proud of yourself is not the same as **bragging** about yourself. Bragging is telling others how good or smart or clever you are. Bragging is putting yourself above other people. That is not a nice thing to do.

Many people in history have felt or shown pride. One of these people was Francis Scott Key. He was a **lawyer**. Key lived when the American **colonies** won their freedom from the British. People were proud to live in a free country.

In 1812, the British attacked Washington, D.C. British troops also fired bombs and rockets at Fort McHenry near Baltimore, Maryland. The fort survived the attack. Francis Scott Key was proud that the Americans had won the battle. He wrote a poem called "The Star-Spangled Banner" to show his pride for his country.

This is a painting of Francis Scott Key looking at Fort McHenry.

Feeling pride is important. When you feel pride, you show others that you feel good about yourself and others. What have you been proud of today?

At Home

- Ask your parents to put your special artwork on display.

- Keep your room clean and neat.

- Teach your brother or sister how to play a game you know.

At School

- Take your time and do your projects and schoolwork neatly.

- Cheer for the winners of school competitions.

- To keep the school looking nice, clean up any messes you make.

In Your Community

- Show visitors your favorite places in your community.

- Fly your country's flag on special holidays.

- Throw your trash in the trash can at the park.

Glossary

bragging (BRAG-ging)
Bragging is talking about how good you are at something.

colonies (KOL-uh-neez)
Colonies are lands ruled by a faraway country.

lawyer (LOY-er)
A lawyer is a person who helps others with the law. A lawyer often speaks for people in court.

Pledge of Allegiance
(PLEJ uv uh-LEE-jents)
The Pledge of Allegiance is a promise to support the United States. It is often recited in school classrooms.

spelling bee (SPEL-ling BEE)
A spelling bee is a contest in which students must spell words correctly.

Index

To Find Out More

Books

Dr. Seuss. *The Big Brag.* New York: Random House, 1998.

Pfister, Marcus. *The Rainbow Fish.* New York: North South Books, 1996.

Spier, Peter (Illustrator). *The Star-Spangled Banner.* New York: Yearling Books, 1992.

Whitcraft, Melissa. *Francis Scott Key (First Book).* Danbury, Conn.: Franklin Watts, 1994.

Web Sites

How to Have Kids Believe in Themselves
http://www.gettingthru.org/kbelieve.htm
For tips on how to feel proud.

Star-Spangled Banner Links
http://www.treefort.org/~rgrogan/web/flag3.htm
To finds pages about Francis Scott Key, "The Star-Spangled Banner," and Fort McHenry.

Welcome to the GreatKids Network
http://www.greatkids.com/index2.html
To read about kids doing things they are proud of.

Note to Parents and Educators

Welcome to Wonder Books®! These books provide text at three different levels for beginning readers to practice and strengthen their reading skills. Additionally, the use of nonfiction text provides readers the valuable opportunity to *read to learn*, not just to learn to read.

These leveled readers allow children to choose books at their level of reading confidence and performance. Nonfiction Level One books offer beginning readers simple language, word choice, and sentence structure as well as a word list. Nonfiction Level Two books feature slightly more difficult vocabulary, longer sentences, and longer total text. In the back of each Nonfiction Level Two book are an index and a list of books and Web sites for finding out more information. Nonfiction Level Three books continue to extend word choice and length of text. In the back of each Nonfiction Level Three book are a glossary, an index, and a list of books and Web sites for further research.

State and national standards in reading and language arts emphasize using nonfiction at all levels of reading development. Wonder Books® fill the historical void in nonfiction material for primary grade readers with the additional benefit of a leveled text.

About the Author

Kathryn Kyle has taught elementary school and writes extensively for children. She lives in Minnesota.